To all those whose imaginations are as boundless as Anne's —K.G.

To my bosom friend and kindred spirit, Alessandra! —G.G.

Text copyright © 2020 by Kallie George
Illustrations copyright © 2020 by Geneviève Godbout

Tundra Books, an imprint of Penguin Random House Canada Young Readers, a Penguin Random House Company

Library and Archives Canada Cataloguing in Publication

Title: If I couldn't be Anne / written by Kallie George ; illustrated by Geneviève Godbout.
Names: George, K. (Kallie), 1983- author. | Godbout, Geneviève, illustrator.
Identifiers: Canadiana (print) 20190149817 | Canadiana (ebook) 20190149825 | ISBN 9781770499287 (hardcover) | ISBN 9781770499294 (EPUB)
Classification: LCC PS8563.E6257 I32 2020 | DDC jC813/.6—dc23

Published simultaneously in the United States of America by Tundra Books of Northern New York, an imprint of Penguin Random House Canada Young Readers, a Penguin Random House Company

Library of Congress Control Number: 2019945230

Acquired by Tara Walker
Edited by Elizabeth Kribs and Jessica Burgess
Designed by Jennifer Griffiths and Emma Dolan
The artwork in this book was rendered in pastels and colored pencils.
The text was set in a typeface based on handlettering by Geneviève Godbout.

Printed and bound in China

www.penguinrandomhouse.ca

1 2 3 4 5   24 23 22 21 20

Penguin
Random House
TUNDRA BOOKS

If I Couldn't Be Anne

INSPIRED BY ANNE OF GREEN GABLES

Written by KALLIE GEORGE

Illustrated by GENEVIÈVE GODBOUT

tundra

If I couldn't be Anne, Anne with an *e* . . .

I'd be a gull—a splendid, swooping one.

Or a rose so I could find out all the lovely things the flowers say.

Or the wind dancing round the treetops,
waving in the ferns and tickling the
lake to make it laugh.

If I couldn't be Anne, Anne with an *e* . . .

I'd be a tightrope walker, breathless and brave.

Or a lily maid, drifting dreamily through summer.

Or a fancy lady,
pouring a perfect cup of tea,
in a grand, grown-uppish way.

If I couldn't be Anne, Anne with an *e* . . .

I'd be an echo, faraway but friendly.

Or an invisible friend who lives in a book,
a kindred spirit to anyone in need.

If I couldn't be Anne, Anne with an *e* . . .

I'd be a dryad, perching in an old pine.

Or a plain little wood elf, hiding under a mushroom.

Or a frost fairy,
flitting through the woods,
turning the trees yellow and red for fall.

If I couldn't be Anne,
Anne with an *e* . . .

I certainly *wouldn't* be a cook
forced to follow a recipe.

And I certainly *wouldn't* have red hair.

Although red is actually divinely beautiful when compared to ghastly green.

But I *would* be . . .

a princess who lives in marble halls.

Or in a palace made of apple blossoms.

Or maybe I'd live in a star—
that lovely clear big one above the dark hill.

And my name would be Cordelia,
since that is a perfectly elegant name.

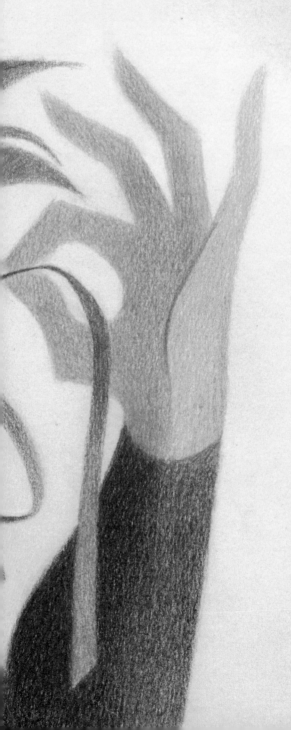

But if I must be Anne, I want to be Anne with an *e*.

And I want to live here — at Green Gables.

Where I will watch the gulls,
smell the roses,
dance round the trees,
have tea with my friends,
walk the rooftops,
recite poetry,
say hello to my echo,
love all the seasons
and wear my perfect
puffed sleeves.

Because some things are even better than imagination.